Bendy Wendy
AND THE (ALMOST) INVISIBLE GENETIC SYNDROME

A story of one tween's diagnosis of Ehlers-Danlos Syndrome / joint hypermobility

BRAD T TINKLE MD PHD   LAURREN DARR

Text and illustrations copyright © 2017 Laurren Darr / Brad T Tinkle / Left Paw Press

Left Paw Press, publishing imprint of Lauren Originals, Inc.

Contact us on our publisher's website at:
www.LeftPawPress.com

ISBN: 978-1-943356-58-4

Library of Congress Control Number: 2017954648

PRINTED IN THE UNITED STATES OF AMERICA

Authors: Brad T Tinkle MD PhD and Laurren Darr

Illustrations: Antonio J. "Nunoh" Díaz

Wendy is excited to go into middle school because she can FINALLY try out for cheerleading. Her dream for as long as she can remember is to be a cheerleader.

She's always been cheerful, talented, outgoing, and limber. In fact, she's so limber when doing jumps and tumbles that she has the nickname 'Bendy Wendy.'

Tryout day arrives and Wendy is ready! In her routine, she does the splits, jumps, and summersaults. She projects her voice loudly and smiles with enthusiasm. Waiting to find out if she made the squad was like torture.

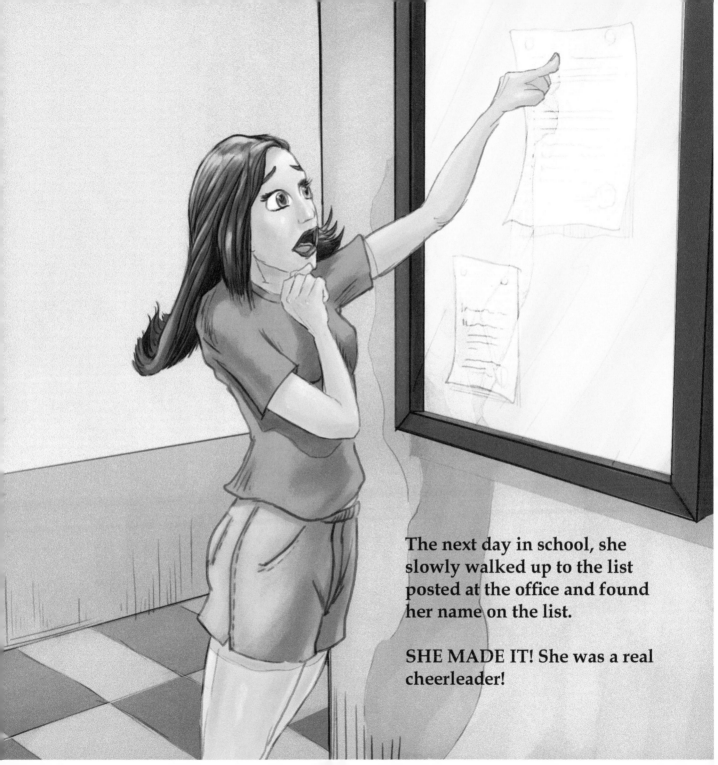

The next day in school, she slowly walked up to the list posted at the office and found her name on the list.

SHE MADE IT! She was a real cheerleader!

Wendy was wholeheartedly committed to being the best. She went to the squad practice every day and cheered at games on the weekends. It was like living a dream.

But, something was happening that she didn't understand. All the exercise was taking a toll on her body. She felt achy after long practices and sometimes she was dizzy. Wendy assumed she would get used to it and chalked it up to her having a new routine.

Things continued to happen and get worse. There were times when she would make a sudden move and her shoulder or hip would pop out of place.

It hurts for a little while, but the joint went easily back in place so she thinks nothing of it since others in her family have similar issues.

Wendy is the 'flyer' that the squad throws up in the air from a pyramid because she can do such a great toe touch. One day she goes way up in the air and comes down to be caught by the other cheerleaders.

When she falls back, she landed on her ankle and twisted it to the point where she can't walk without help. It was devastating and painful.

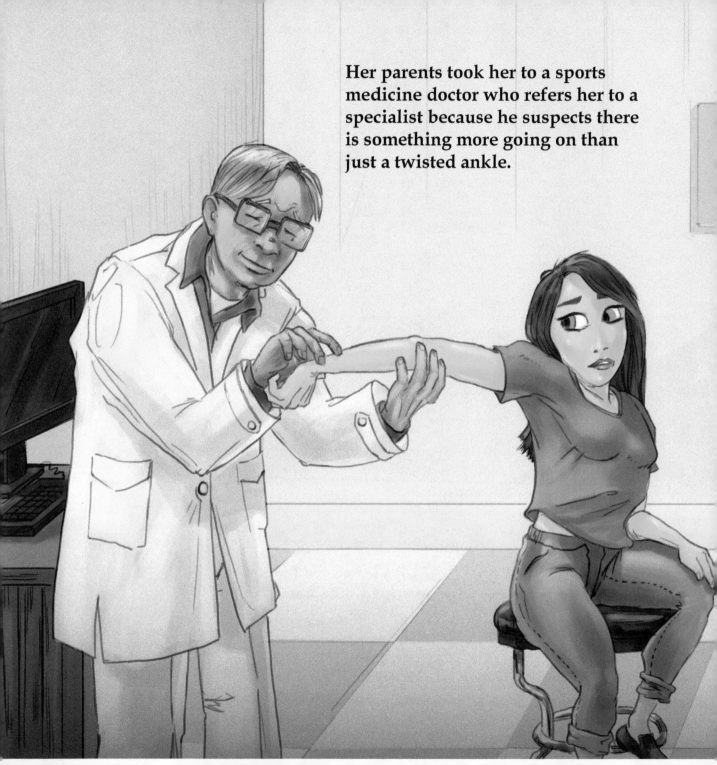

Her parents took her to a sports medicine doctor who refers her to a specialist because he suspects there is something more going on than just a twisted ankle.

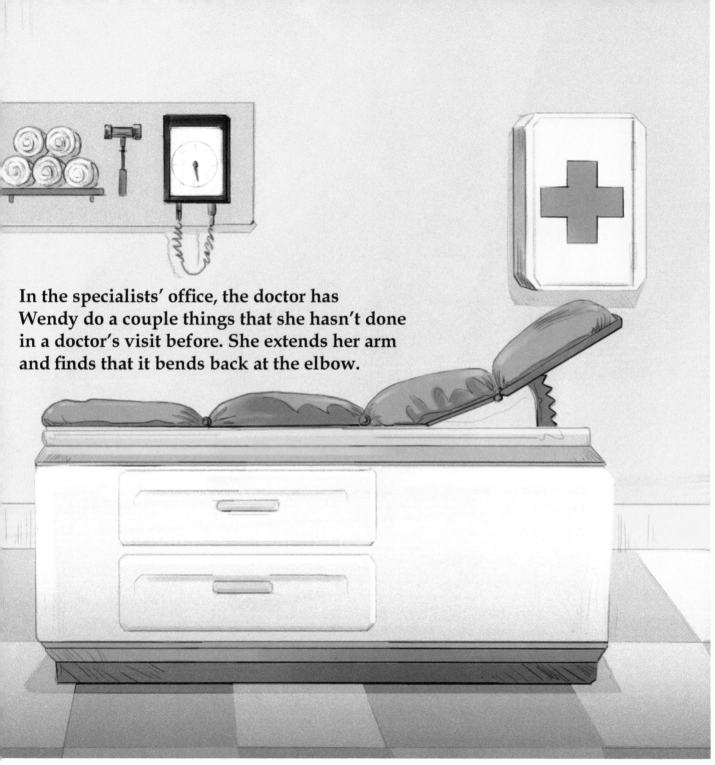

In the specialists' office, the doctor has Wendy do a couple things that she hasn't done in a doctor's visit before. She extends her arm and finds that it bends back at the elbow.

She stands straight up and notices that her legs bow back, much more so than most of her friends.

The doctor takes a bit of her skin and lifts it from her arm and sees that it is 'stretchy.'

After a few other things and conversation on family history with her parents, the doctor says that Wendy has a form of joint hypermobility known as Ehlers-Danlos Syndrome.

They had never heard of this before, but when the doctor talked about the symptoms, it all made sense. Some of the things he mentioned were joints popping out of place, joint pain, bruising easily, getting tired easily, and losing balance or being called "clumsy."

Wendy was afraid the doctor was going to tell her she had to quit cheerleading. That would break her heart.

Luckily, there was good news. She could stay on the squad if she worked on keeping her joints in good shape.

This meant doing exercises.

She had to learn to keep her knees and elbows from bending backwards. This actually made her look better when cheering.

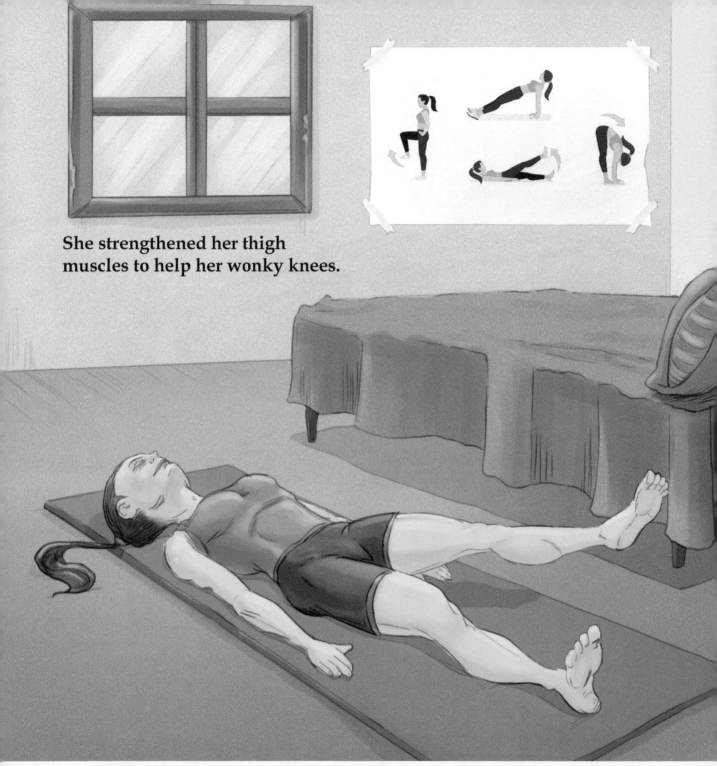

She strengthened her thigh
muscles to help her wonky knees.

Wendy worked on having better posture when sitting and standing to help her back.

She had a routine of stretches to help lower the pain in her muscles.

The family found out that Wendy's lightheadedness to the point she felt faint happened when her heart was racing.

To be safe, they saw a cardiologist who explained that she mainly needed to keep hydrated, include more salt in her diet, and have drinks with electrolytes at practice and games.

While Wendy was working on her strengthening, she had to use ankle braces when she was cheerleading or felt her ankles were hurting.

Wendy was so relieved that, with some extra effort and a doctor's note to her coach that she could continue cheering. Since that was her dream from the time she was a little girl, she dedicated herself to keeping her joints healthy and learning to live with her (almost) invisible genetic syndrome.

CAT & DOG BREEDS FASHION FITTING GUIDE

Laurren Darr

www.PetFashionProfessionals.com

LEFT PAW Press ! Proudly Sponsors

Zachary Tinkle

LORZ Motorsports

Pro Late Model Stock Car Driver

53

2018 Series

CRA POWERED BY JEGS
CHAMPION RACING ASSOCIATION

Tinkle Family Racing

LEFT PAW Press !

SIMPSON

BTT consulting

michele v. wagner

DIY MARKETING .tv

International Association of
PET FASHION PROFESSIONALS

Get the most comprehensive dog fashion illustrations set along with design considerations in the Dog Breeds Pet Fashion Illustration Encyclopedia book set. Includes all of the AKC breeds separated by the seven breed groups.

Companion Coloring Books
ALSO AVAILABLE

www.PetFashionProfessionals.com

RELIEVE STRESS BY COLORING

Keep checking **LeftPawPress.com** for even more pet-related mandala coloring books.

PUG CHILDREN'S FAIRY TALE SERIES
BOOKS ARE AVAILABLE IN COLOR
AND COLORING BOOK VERSIONS

Pug Benji and the ... Coloring Book
Story Adaptation by: Laurren Darr
Illustrated by Florina Boldi
Pug Fairy Tale Series

Li'l Red Riding ... Coloring Book
Story A... Laurren ...
Florin...

Mother Pug Rhym... Coloring Book
Pug Fairy Tale Series

Pug in Bo... Coloring Book
Pug Fairy Tale Series

The Three Li'l Pugs Coloring Book
Story Adaptation by: Laurren Darr
Illustrated by Florina Boldi

Pug Benji and the Bea...
Story Adaptation by: Laurren Darr
Illustrated by Florina Boldi
Pug Fairy Tale Series

Li'l Red Riding Pu...
Pug Fairy Tale Series

Mother Pug Rhy...
Pug Fairy Tale Seri...

Pug in Bo...
Story A... Lai...
Illustr... Florin...
Pug Fairy Tale Series

The Three Li'l Pugs
Story Adaptation by: Laurren Darr
Illustrated by Florina Boldi
Pug Fairy Tale Series

LEFT PAW Press!

www.LeftPawPress.com

Learn about the roots of Laurren's plumb pug craziness and obsession with pet fashion in this children's book that will teach about the love of dog, pet rescue, and the unbreakable bonds between humans and their pets.

Lipstick On A Pug won the 2015 Children's Book of the Year Maxwell Medallion from the Dog Writers Association of America.

Also available in coloring book format

TAMBIÉN EN ESPAÑOL

Pet Fashion Industry Patterns
by
Laurren Darr

Written based on many years of observations of the pet fashion industry, is this uniquely stylish business trend book from International Association of Pet Fashion Professionals founder, Laurren Darr. It's broken into four enlightening sections that provide valuable insights to those seeking an understanding of pet fashion industry developments. These sections include Pet Trends, Lifestyle Trends, Market Trends, and Micro Trends.

Readers will find that this book is a lot of information in a concise, informative, and creative package. Each chapter is artfully named to be remarkable. Titles include *Purr-fect Fashion, Chicks Dig It, Furbulous Fashion Meets Function, Tail Wagging Markets, Eco-Fido, Paw-er Shopping, and Cosmopawlitan Pets.*

Some of the features that you'll find are:

✓ Black and white photos of some of the most fashionable cities in the world with interesting factoids about each
✓ Fabulous fashion illustrations demonstrating the topic that is discussed in each chapter.
Statistics and facts on pets, business, and the pet industry highlighted throughout.
✓

About Brad T Tinkle

Brad T Tinkle, M.D., Ph.D., is the Medical Director of Clinical Genetics at Advocate Children's Hospital in the Chicago, Illinois area.

Previously, Dr. Tinkle served as a clinical and clinical molecular geneticist at Cincinnati Children's Hospital Medical Center (CCHMC). Dr. Brad, as he's called by many of his patients, specializes in caring for individuals with heritable connective tissue disorders such as Ehlers-Danlos syndromes, Marfan syndrome, osteogenesis imperfecta, and achondroplasia among the many. While at CCHMC, he served as director of the Skeletal Dysplasia Center, co-director of the Marfan/ Ehlers-Danlos syndrome clinic, as well as director of the Connective Tissue Clinics. In addition, he served as associate director in the Clinical Molecular Genetics Laboratory.

He earned a Bachelor's in Science for Engineering (BSE) in genetic engineering from Purdue University in 1989 and received his Ph.D. in Human Genetics from the George Washington University in the District of Columbia in 1995. Dr. Brad then attended medical school at Indiana University and completed a pediatric/clinical genetics residency at CCHMC. He also finished a fellowship in clinical molecular genetics at CCHMC following residency. Currently, Dr. Tinkle is board certified in pediatrics and clinical genetics.

He currently serves on the Professional Advisory Network of the Ehlers-Danlos Society. Dr. Tinkle has authored medical articles, book chapters, and two books on EDS: "Issues and Management of Joint Hypermobility.." (2008) and "The Joint Hypermobility Handbook" (2010) and is internationally recognized as an expert in the care and management of those with EDS. The Ehlers-Danlos Society awarded Tinkle with the Community Choice Award in 2016. In 2017, he served as editor as well as author and co-author of a supplement for the American Journal of Medical Genetics titled "The Ehlers-Danlos Syndromes: Reports from the International Consortium on the Ehlers-Danlos Syndromes." The Ehlers-Danlos Society honored Dr. Tinkle in 2017 with a Lifetime Achievement Award.

About Laurren Darr

Laurren Darr has been a plumb-pug-crazy, animal-loving, pet fashionologist and creative since childhood. She immerses herself in expression through writing and art including creating the publishing imprint Left Paw Press in 2008.

Laurren also happens to be the wife to her geneticist co-author Dr. Brad T Tinkle. She and Dr. Brad combined their experience and skill sets to create "Bendy Wendy and the (Almost) Invisible Genetic Syndrome... A story of one tween's diagnosis of Ehlers-Danlos Syndrome / joint hypermobility" to fill an area that they both felt needed addressing after many conversations with patients and families afflicted with Ehlers-Danlos Syndrome / joint hypermobility.

Laurren has won over forty marketing awards for her background in creating advertising and marketing campaigns for companies and clients of all sizes and is a #1 best-selling author. Her children's book, Lipstick On A Pug, won the Maxwell Medallion from the Dog Writers Association of America in 2015 and was named Children's Book of the Year. In 2016, her PugDala Coloring Book also won a Maxwell Medallion.

In August 2013, Laurren combined her marketing experience and lifelong love of pet fashionology to launch International Association of Pet Fashion Professionals, an organization created to provide tools to the pet fashion industry. She's been named a "Paw-er Woman" by the Fidose of Reality blog and was a 2015 &16 finalist for Pet Industry Woman of the Year by Women In The Pet Industry. Laurren also completed her pet fashion certification from FIT (Fashion Institute of Technology).

Laurren's busy home is filled with her geneticist husband, her son, Zachary Tinkle, (who is a rising stock car racing star), and her fabulously fashionable fawn pug, Bella.

CPSIA information can be obtained
at www.ICGtesting.com
Printed in the USA
LVHW070616140820
663095LV00016B/1788

9 781943 356584